Snowflake Hollow - Part 10

12 Days of Christmas, Volume 10

Lexy Timms

Published by Dark Shadow Publishing, 2021.

SNOWFLAKE HOLLOW

12 DAYS OF CHRISTMAS
PART TEN

USA TODAY BESTSELLING AUTHOR

LEXY TIMMS

Snowflake
HOLLOW
12 DAYS OF CHRISTMAS
Part Ten
USA TODAY BESTSELLING AUTHOR
LEXY TIMMS

12 Days of Christmas Series

Find Lexy Timms:

LEXY TIMMS NEWSLETTER:
https://www.lexytimms.com/newsletter
Lexy Timms Facebook Page:
https://www.facebook.com/SavingForever
Lexy Timms Website:
http://www.lexytimms.com

Want to read more...
For **FREE?**
Sign up for Lexy Timms' newsletter
And she'll send you updates on new releases, ARC copies of books and
a whole lotta fun!
Sign up for news and updates!
https://www.lexytimms.com/newsletter

Snow Flake Hollow

YOU ARE THE GREATEST gift I could wish for this Christmas...

She's not the biggest fan of Christmas – which is akin to a major sin in the little town of Snowflake Hollow. And with a name like Holly White, it's fitting that she owns the only B&B in town. The whole season is a huge deal, and the people coming to stay at the B&B are paying a premium to get the ultimate festive experience. She's trying to keep the guests busy, but Hank the Handyman just broke his leg trying to hang the lights. Now she has to figure out how to make the holiday festivities happen all by herself.

Enter Lawson Lane.

Mister tall, dark and handsome, has come home to see his mother over the holidays, and is surprised to see Holly as the owner of the B&B. When he notices her struggling to get things done, he offers a helping hand. Seeing Holly again and enjoying the holidays might take a Christmas miracle—or he might end up with a lump of coal in his stocking.

It's 12 days of festive fun, what could possibly go wrong?

Lexy Timms brings you a Christmas holiday romance with 12 days of Christmas – each part of the story releasing like opening an advent calendar! Join in the holiday spirit with a festive read and some laughs to get you into the Christmas season.

Chapter Fifty-Five

Lawson

I woke up with the old excitement filling my bones and a smile on my face. It was only a few days until Christmas, and everything was getting more festive around the bed and breakfast. And to top it off, Holly was the one in the lead of almost all of it.

It was difficult for her, I could tell. The Christmas spirit wasn't natural to her, and she didn't have much experience with it, but she was giving it one hell of a try. While it took extra work for her, it was more meaningful in a way because of it. She was clearly working against years of thinking one way and trying to open herself up to something new. And that something new was bringing her joy when she let it.

The house was absolutely covered in decorations for one thing. There were garlands wrapped around the railing of the stairs and lights along the steps themselves. Peppermint candles burned in most of the open spaces, and where they weren't gingerbread ones were. That was when there wasn't the smell of something freshly baking, usually because I had tossed it in.

Music was generally playing downstairs during the daytime and evening hours. Soft, low-volume sounds of Christmas carols—almost all the upbeat ones and a handful of the slower ones—filled the place with sound. Guests could be seen tapping their feet or humming along with the songs as they went about their day, and I even caught Holly singing under her breath a few times.

Snowfall outside, warm wonderful smells inside. It was Christmas in Snowflake Hollow.

The excitement was building in me like a little kid. I loved all of this, more than I could express to Holly or anyone else. It filled me with a kind of positive energy that could have moved the Statue of Liberty around New York City if I had some of that pink Ghostbusters' goo.

I loved all of it. The silly, cheesy nature of the holiday movies, the overload of peppermint and sugar cookies, the sappy songs about going home... all of it was like nectar to me. It reminded me of better times, of more innocent moments of my life when nothing mattered in the world other than how much fun I was going to have the next day.

Days when I didn't worry as much about my mother.

I went over to see her a few times, and we were calling each other fairly frequently. There was some guilt about how I had wrapped myself up with Holly and was spending so much time helping her out and doing things at the bed and breakfast, but Mom was always so supportive. She would wave it off and tell me I needed to focus on me. She wasn't going anywhere yet.

I hated when she said 'yet'. I knew she didn't mean it that way, but every time she did it, it was a reminder that her time on Earth had a clock that was ticking down. And that there wasn't a lot of that time left. But she tried to keep me focused on positive things: I was there, and she loved seeing me, and that I was having fun being back home for a little while.

I hadn't told her much about Holly, but what I had I got the impression she knew how to read in to. She was my mother, after all, and knew more than anyone else what made me tick. When I talked about Holly I tried to keep things vague and distant, but I knew she saw the excitement in my eyes and heard it in my voice. There was no avoiding it.

We would also talk about Christmases when I was a kid. Times where she would come outside with me and we would build a snowman and go sledding. We laughed about the time I slid down a hill too fast and ended up crashing into a cheap playhouse, smashing it to bits. I spent the rest of the winter rebuilding that thing for the neighbors so their granddaughter had her place back. I wasn't entirely sure she even knew what happened to it, but I did it for her anyway.

Snow days were the best back then, and I was determined to have it be just as good for the kids staying at the bed and breakfast now. I would wake up early and go outside, grabbing sleds and shovels, and head out to the open fields to run free with the other kids in the neighborhood. After our sledding adventure, I had pulled the sleds away from the garage and stuffed them under the porch. I hoped they would be visible enough that anyone wanting to use them could see them.

Our snowman was going strong outside, too. The long scarf had blown in the wind and nearly come off a few times, but the other guests would always help fix him, too. Someone had added a top hat, from where I didn't know, and the stick we had stuck in to be his arm was replaced with a thicker one that had branches sticking out that looked like he was waving jauntily.

The text message that came in as I was getting dressed only added to the excitement. An idea had formed immediately, and I knew just what I wanted to do today. If there was anything that could push Holly over the edge into full-on Christmas nerd, this might be it. I just hoped she would go with me on it. I knew there was still lots to do around the place, and keeping up with the guests was her top priority, but I felt like my plan would be super rewarding for both of us.

I opened the top drawer of the dresser in my room and smiled. I put on the silly Christmas tree socks that were lying on top and laughed at how wonderfully silly they looked. I had bought them on a lark last year when I saw them in a store a few days after Christmas. Thankfully, I had remembered to throw them into my bag and bring them with me. Finally, I slipped on sneakers and went downstairs. Usually, first thing in the morning, I could be found with my slippers still on, but this time I wanted to be ready to move. I didn't want to give Holly any excuse not to get going, including me needing a few minutes to get ready.

The lights were on downstairs, and the aroma of coffee filled the dining room area, though I didn't hear the shuffling of anyone down there. Usually, only the elderly guests were up before I went down to make the pots of coffee, but apparently someone beat me down there, even if they weren't milling around. As I rounded the corner of the kitchen, I saw who it was.

Holly was sitting in the floor of the kitchen, her legs crossed at the ankles but her legs bowed. A large mixing bowl was between her thighs and a heavy wooden spoon stuck inside. She looked like she was staring down into the bowl, looking for the answers to the universe. I stared at her for a moment before she seemed to notice I was there and looked up only briefly.

The bowl was full of dough. Big, thick, heavy dough. The oven beeped, indicating it had preheated to a pre-determined temperature, and I looked questioningly from it to Holly. What in the heck was she up to? Usually she waited for me before she tried anything with the oven.

"What exactly is going on here?" I asked, pulling a mug down and grabbing the pot of coffee.

"Me and the dough are coming to an understanding," she said.

I laughed at that and reached down to kiss her on the top of her head before sitting in one of the chairs by the kitchen table.

"Why do you and the dough have to come to an understanding, sitting in the floor of the kitchen?" I asked.

"Because I was mixing it," she said. "And I couldn't get a good enough grip on it. So, I tried holding it tight to my chest, but that didn't really work either. Then I figured I could keep it between my thighs, but there wasn't enough room on the chair, so..."

"So, you ended up on the floor," I said.

"Yup," she said. "I ended up on the floor. Nice socks, by the way."

I beamed.

"Thank you. They have little bells on them."

"I can see that. And hear it," she said. "You jangled all the way down the stairs."

"At least I didn't surprise you," I said.

"True," she said. "I wouldn't want to get startled and throw my dough on the floor or anything. We just need to get to a good place with each other and have some understanding about not being burned to be-jesus."

"Well, maybe you should put the dough in the fridge to think for a little while and make something simpler for breakfast," I said. "Like waffles. Or cereal."

"That sounds like we have a Christmas activity scheduled for the day," she said.

I grinned.

"You don't have to say it like that," I said. "Besides, it's not a Christmas activity, per se. It's a Christmas mission."

"Like the military?" she asked. "I don't know if I have enough Christmas spirit to invade another town or anything. Also, that seems to be slightly against the spirit of the holiday, I would think."

"Not quite like the military," I said. "But an important mission nonetheless."

"All right, I'll bite," she said. "What is it we need to do? And please tell me it doesn't involve wearing fatigues."

"No fatigues," I said. "Unless maybe you want to for some reason. But I think you could get by with anything."

"Good," she said.

"Do you remember that mailbox I put up outside the Children's Hospital?" I asked.

"The day we went to the market? Yeah, why?" she asked.

"Well, I just got a message from one of the people working over there."

"Oh no, is something wrong with the mailbox? Did some stupid kids hit it with a bat or something?" she asked, a concerned expression on her face.

"No," I said, taking a deep sip of my coffee and shaking my head. "That's not something that happens much in Snowflake Hollow. No, the mailbox is fine."

"Then what about it?" she asked.

"Apparently, some of the little patients up there and their siblings took the mailbox to heart. There are a bunch of letters to Santa inside."

"Really?" she asked

I nodded.

"They messaged me this morning and asked what I thought they should do with them."

Chapter Fifty-Six

Holly

I didn't even hesitate.

"Absolutely," I said. "One hundred percent. Let's do it."

Lawson grinned the boyish grin he got when he started getting excited for something, and I felt my heart clench. There was just something so adorable about him when he smiled like that, something so attractive. He was a gorgeous man, there was no doubt about that, but when he showed his excitement like that it was even more pronounced.

He stood, putting his mug of coffee down on the table, and opened his arms. I had a harder time getting to my feet, considering I was on the floor and had a giant mixing bowl of dough in between my legs, but I made the effort anyway and moved toward him. He pulled me into his arms tight and I felt myself melt into his chest. I leaned my face up and he pressed a kiss to my lips, and what little control I had left went away as I sank into him.

"I think," he said, "you might have just found a bit of the Christmas spirit after all."

"Maybe," I said. "Maybe it's just coming from you."

"Either way, I'm happy," he laughed, kissing me again.

"I bet you are," I said.

"Come on, let's wrap this up and stick it in the fridge."

I pulled the plastic wrap from the shelf where it had been moved to since we were using it so often lately, and pulled out far more of it than I needed for the bowl. I tried rerolling it, but no matter how many times

I try that and it doesn't work, I'm still a sucker for it the next time and go through the same frustrating realization. Finally, I just cut off what I needed using the little blades that always seemed to tear the plastic rather than cut it, and wrapped it over the bowl.

Lawson watched me patiently as I fought with the plastic wrap and then finally got the dough in the refrigerator. He had one arm rested on the other, crossed over him, his chin in his hands. His eyes gave off the impression that he was very amused.

"What?"

"Just you," he said, shaking his head a little. "You have to be the cutest person in the history of the world. That's all."

"Oh, well," I said, looking for some kind of comeback and finding none. "Yes."

"Let's get going," he said. "I'll go start the car, you grab your coat and boots."

He jogged off excitedly, grabbing his coat off the coatrack and slipping it on. The cold air from outside blew in as he opened the door and I shivered. I was going to need more than the yoga pants and sweater combo I was rocking that morning.

Jogging upstairs, I grabbed some fleece-lined jeans and a pair of boots and put them on quickly, then booked for the door. My coat was warm on account of the coat rack being close to the fireplace, and I greatly enjoyed sliding it on and bundling up. By the time I had the door open and got to the car, Lawson was sitting in the driver's seat, unbuttoning his top button. The heater was blowing hard. I must have taken a bit longer than I thought.

The hospital wasn't too far away, and when we got there I saw that the little mailbox he had stuck outside was completely cleared of snow. It was like someone had gone out there specifically to make sure it was visible, even though they didn't bother to do the same with the real mailbox a few feet away.

"Looks like someone moved it," Lawson said. "I put it a little further out."

"Weird," I said, opening the door of the car after he parked and turned off the ignition. I kind of wanted to stay there in the cab while it was still warm and toasty, but I knew the hospital should be comfortable, too. I could deal with a few dozen feet of snow.

We made our way to the front door and the electric sensor picked us up and opened it for us. Standing in the little vestibule between the sets of doors, I could see a rather tall, heavyset woman inside by the check-in desk. She was older, blonde, and very well put-together. She had the look of a woman in charge. She looked up and saw Lawson and waved.

"Oh, there's Rachael; she's one of the directors of the hospital," he said, waving back. I joined him in waving, and when our boots were thoroughly stamped of all the snow we could get off of them we opened the door into the main lobby.

The building felt rather small, only two floors, but stretching back a good ways so it took up most of the block. It was deceiving a bit in how large it was, and as the only children's hospital for a couple of counties it was probably full rather often.

Rachael crossed the distance between us at a trot and threw her arms around Lawson for a big hug. It was a surprising amount of emotion for a woman that looked as put together as her. But the smile on her face said volumes. She adored Lawson.

"It's so good to see you," she said. "Thank you for coming down. Who's your friend?"

"This is Holly White," he said, and I held out my hand for a shake.

"Oh, we don't shake here," she said, pulling me in for a hug, too. My face squished against her massive bosom and I laughed. She gave great hugs.

"Nice to meet you," I said.

"Likewise," she said. "Thank you both for coming by."

"Of course," I said.

"So tell us what's going on," Lawson said.

"Come on in first," she said. "Let's get where it's warm. Can I get you a coffee? Tea?"

"Coffee please," Lawson said. "I only had one cup this morning."

"And you?" the woman asked, looking at me.

"Oh, I had like four. I'm good," I said. "I was at war with a bowl of dough, so I caffeinated myself quite well."

"Ah," she said. "Well, when one is at war with baking, it is best to stay well-caffeinated."

She ran off, presumably to a kitchenette or breakroom somewhere, and I laughed.

"I like her," I said.

"So do I," Lawson said. "I've donated to this Children's Hospital for years. I've known Rachael for a long time."

"Oh," I said.

Another thing that I never knew. And another thing to add to the list of reasons Lawson was incredible. I was wondering if I was going to have to start writing them down. Maybe I could make a book? Probably no one would believe any of it if I did.

"Here we go," she said, coming back out with a mug in one hand and a bottle of water and a bag in the other. "I couldn't just not bring you something."

"Thank you," I said, smiling and taking the water bottle. "Water sounds amazing right now, actually."

She ushered us to a couple of couches by a large fireplace. There was no fire going in the fireplace, but the hospital had that slight hint of warmth that hospitals tended to have at winter. Cold does something to kill germs I had heard once, which was probably why it wasn't really warm, but at least it was better than outside.

"So," she said, sitting down on the edge of one of the couches while Lawson sat next to me. Her eyes shifted over to him and how close we were sitting, but she didn't say anything. She noticed, though. She most certainly noticed. "I have this."

She handed over the bag, and I opened it. Inside were dozens of envelopes and folded-up pieces of paper. Some of the kids had simply written Santa's name on the outside of the sheet and stuck it in the mailbox.

"This is adorable," I said.

Rachael smiled thinly and nodded.

"Yes, it is. I didn't really expect that, since most of the children stay in their rooms. But occasionally either their parents or the nurses will take them out for walks around the courtyard, and when it snowed we brought many of them out for a moment. It was just such a magical moment."

"It was," I agreed.

"So, they put all these in the mailbox?" Lawson asked.

"I didn't know they did, but yes," she said. "I actually brought the whole thing inside to use as a decoration. We throw them a Christmas party every year inside the lobby. It's really rather small, but it's something that helps them by giving them something to look forward to and brighten up what can be a very sad time of year for them."

"I'm sure," I said.

"This year has been especially hard," she continued. "We have a lot more patients than in years past. It's difficult on all of us, really, the entire staff and everyone, but we still wanted our Christmas party to be as special as possible. Unfortunately, some of our decorations were getting a little beat up and I thought it would be nice to replace some of them with the mailbox. It's just so cute.

"Anyway, I brought it in, and it jostled a bit and a letter fell out. I noticed what it was and opened the box to find all these. When I realized what they had done I knew I couldn't keep it inside, and brought it back out but took the envelopes with me."

"Do you think there are any more letters out there?" he asked.

"It's possible," she said. "I don't know. I meant to bring it in again as a decoration now that the party is here."

"Wait, when is the party?" Lawson asked.

"Tonight," she said, wringing her hands a bit. "I know, it all kind of caught up to us really quickly. We didn't know about the letters until yesterday, and by then it was too late to do anything about them. We are going to be here working all night as it is, just trying to keep up, and that's still with all of us doing what we can to take some time and decorate and then throw the party."

"Hey, it's okay," Lawson said, noticing she was getting a little upset. He held out his hand and touched her shoulder. She seemed to calm a little.

"What do you need?" I asked.

"I honestly don't know," she said. "I hate to ask anyone for anything, but you know how the funding is." Lawson nodded solemnly. "We just don't have the budget to do much, and what you see is about all we had."

The room was decorated, though it was a bit light. A lot of the decorations looked either very old or cheap, like from a dollar store. The others were hand-made and of varying quality. There was a gorgeous Christmas quilt hung on a wall that looked like it had been made years before, but was painstakingly done.

"So, the party is tonight," I said. "What time?"

"Well, it's children, so it's supposed to be pretty early. We usually aim for six or so, but seven would work, too."

"Seven," Lawson said. "Doesn't give us much time, but that's fine."

"Seriously, anything you can do," she said. "Even if it's just helping us decorate or bake or something. We just want this to be as special as we possibly can for them, and I just don't know how it's going to go."

I smiled, reaching out and taking one of her hands hand in mine and making strong eye contact with her. Tears brimmed in the corners of her hazel eyes and she batted them away with a painted red fingernail.

"I promise you," I said, "it will be as special as you want it to be."

Chapter Fifty-Seven

Lawson

Watching Holly listen to and talk to Rachael made my heart full in a way that I had never experienced before. She was so sincere, so compassionate, a depth of emotion that I wasn't even aware of coming up to the surface and allowing for her to comfort this woman and tell her that it would be okay. That we would pick up the slack that they needed to give these kids a good Christmas.

I knew that meant a lot of pressure, but I didn't care. This was what the spirit of Christmas was really all about. Giving when you could give, and doing so without any expectation of reward.

"Are you sure?" Rachael asked, her brow furrowed. It was a risk, letting us take this on. We didn't work there. We weren't even volunteers. Technically, I donated money every year, and I had brought the mailbox, but that was the extent of my involvement up to now.

"Yes," Holly said. "Absolutely. You leave it to us."

Rachael smiled and we sat with her for a few more minutes, discussing their plans for the evening. I needed to know as much as I could about what they planned, as I had some ideas of how to make the evening special, but I kept getting distracted watching Holly. She was being so sweet, so caring with Rachael. It made me feel even stronger about her than I thought I did already.

My ears perked up when I heard my name, and I looked at the expectant eyes of Rachael.

"I'm sorry, I was lost in thought," I said. "What was that?"

"I said that I would love it if you could bring the mailbox in for me again," Rachael said. "My back has been bothering me and I still have so many decorations left to put up."

"Sure," I said. "I'll go get it now."

"Is there anything I can help you put up?" Holly asked as I started toward the door.

"Actually, there is," Rachael said. "Let me go fetch the ladder."

I walked outside, grinning. Holly was really getting into the spirit of things. Maybe it was Christmas, maybe it was me, or maybe it was just that she could see how obviously Rachael needed help and how much good it would do. The children's hospital was known for being very lenient about getting paid by the families, reaching out to their network of donors and local companies to help pay bills that families had, and trying to get doctors to volunteer their time.

When my business had first kicked off, becoming successful to a point where I had money to do something with, it was one of the first things I wanted to do with it. I wanted to help the Children's Hospital monetarily, especially since I knew that was probably the easiest way to help. So often places like that would get overloads of donations and volunteers, but what they really needed was money. Money made things happen.

But today was different. Not only did they need the financial help that I knew I could provide in a pinch, but they also needed manpower. Rachael couldn't do it all on her own, even though I knew she would try. Holly and I could pick up some of that slack, though, and not only could we but I felt compelled to do it. From the way she was reacting in there, listening to Rachael, I got the impression Holly did, too.

It was a remarkable turnaround for her. Not that I didn't think she was charitable or helpful before, but I don't think she would have gone out of her way to find someone to help. If she had come across something to donate to or something like that, sure, she wouldn't think twice about donating. But this was something different. We both felt it. She was reaching out in the spirit of the holiday, and helping other people. I was proud of her.

I was in awe of her.

The mailbox resting on my shoulder, I went back inside to find Holly perched on top of a ladder, putting a star on the top of a Christmas tree that had seemingly appeared from nowhere. I stopped, watching them for a moment before they noticed me and Holly sat on the top step, in clear violation of OSHA rules.

"Where did that come from?" I asked.

"We had it in the break room," Rachael said. "It was just sitting in the corner, unadorned, waiting for me to bring it out here. But I'm no good on ladders, and I couldn't seem to get anyone else to stop long enough to put the star up there. I think I can handle the rest."

She wasn't lying. Rachael was a large woman, in every respect of the word. I had no problem believing that she could hang most of the ornaments high up on the tree with ease. But it was also a tall tree, and even she couldn't reach the top. Holly came down the ladder and pushed it off to the side, grabbing an open box that revealed itself to be full of ornaments.

"Come on," Holly said. "Help us toss some of these ornaments on so she doesn't have to."

Grinning, I walked up to her and took some of the shiny red balls from the box, thankful that they already had the hooks on them. Holly gleefully began hanging green ones at intervals between where I hung red ones, and it became a game of her following me around the tree. It was, again, a contrast to decorating at the bed and breakfast. While she had fun doing that, this was another level of silliness that she had never exhibited before. I loved it.

When we had put about half the ornaments on, I glanced at my watch and set the box down. Holly looked over her shoulder at me and then pulled out her phone, checking the time.

"Looks like we need to get going," I said. "If we're going to do what I want to do, we need to get a move on."

"Of course," Rachael said. "Thank you both so much for your help. It will be a lot easier to finish this now that I don't have to worry about climbing a ladder." She paused, looking at the tree for a moment. "Wait. You two should be here when I turn on the lights. It's not so much of a 'grand' illumination, but it's what I've got. A medium illumination, I guess."

We waited for a moment while she plugged the tree in and then stood by the little switch on the floor. With a fake drumroll, she stepped on the switch and the tree light up with red, green, and white lights. They twinkled and the light bounced off the shiny ornaments, giving the room a glow even in the sunlight. I smiled, then looked at Holly who was smiling, too. I thought I even saw a bit of mist in her eyes.

With an idea of our tight timeframe in mind, Holly and I said our goodbyes and headed for the car, the bag of letters in Holly's hand. When we got into the car, she exhaled.

"This is going to be tough," she said. "But I think we should go back to the house and look through these before we do anything else."

"I agree," I said. "Thankfully it's still early, and no one in town shuts down until Christmas Day. We have a little bit of a window here."

I drove us back to the bed and breakfast and we went inside, Holly to the floor of the main room and me into the kitchen to grab another coffee for me and a cocoa for Holly. Peppermints went into both. I would probably have some cocoa myself before we left, but I felt like an extra jolt of coffee getting me somewhere in the neighborhood of where Holly was would be helpful.

Holly was sitting cross-legged on the floor and I joined her, pushing the table back a bit to give us room. With the fire on one side of us and the table on the other, we created a kind of workstation. Holly stacked up the letters and gave me half and we put them on the table, working them from there to our hands and then to our other side as we organized them by what they said.

Some of them were quite funny. The kids that had written them either didn't really have the hang of what writing to Santa was, or they were older and were skeptical and it came through in their letter. One asked for a bunch of bananas along with his toys, not because of any deep love of bananas but because he didn't tell anyone else about it and it would be the only way he could be sure it was really Santa and not his parents.

Other letters weren't so funny. They were absolutely heartbreaking, and I would either catch Holly sniffling as she read one or she would see me frozen, fighting back tears. I had one of those letters in my hand when she laughed loudly, and noticed that I wasn't as jovial.

"Oh no," she said. "What's going on with yours?"

"He has terminal cancer," I said. "He just wants his parents to be happy. That's it. It's the whole letter. He just wants his parents to be happy and his little brother to get to be healthy his whole life."

"Oh gosh," Holly said, her face bunching up much in the same manner I was sure mine was, too.

"I don't know how to help this kid," I said.

"You can't," she said. "Not directly. But you can make sure his parents are able to see him have a good time at this party tonight. And, in a way, that will be fulfilling part of it."

I nodded, trying to accept that. It was going to be hard. For as fun as the night could be, to know that there were kids with such simple, wholesome, and un-giveable things that were on their list would haunt me. I just had to do as much as I could.

"Here's one," I said, pulling another letter from the stack. It had a giant drawing of what I assumed to be an elf on the front. "Dear Santa, I know you can't be real. It doesn't make sense. Fat men can't come down chimneys. It's a fact. But if you are real, then you shouldn't have a problem bringing me a bunch of comic books, preferably *Iron Man*. Thanks. Jerome."

"Jerome is having trouble with his own Christmas spirit it seems," Holly said.

"Well, we can fix that. There's a comic shop in town," I said. "It's not far from the hospital actually."

"Would they carry *Iron Man*?" she asked.

I paused for a moment, looking at her.

"Would they carry one of the most popular comics of all time, especially after it was revived in the single- most financially successful film series of all time? Yes. Yes, I think they will carry it."

"I didn't know," she said, shrugging and giggling. "I haven't seen the movies, either."

"Wait, what?" I asked. "You haven't seen any of them? That has to change. We have a marathon to do."

"Aren't there, like, twenty of them?" she asked.

"Something like that, if you add all of them up. Then there are the TV series episodes. It's a lot."

"So, not something we could fit in before Christmas," she asked.

"No, but I'm sure we can figure out a time to get them all in," I said. We paused as we smiled at each other, her cheeks blushing and her eyes sparkling. "But for now, we need to get a move on. We have a bunch of sick kids counting on us."

Chapter Fifty-Eight

Holly

I would be lying if I said a little part of me wasn't excited just to go shopping with Lawson in the little shops on Main Street.

Being out and about with him, in the craze of last-minute Christmas shoppers, walking through the winter wonderland that was Snowflake Hollow, was like a dream. We parked on one of the side streets and got out to walk along the shops, knowing we could always bring stuff back to the car and stuff it in if it was too much to carry around.

I didn't much care where we started. I wasn't shopping for me, so my mission was a little different than perhaps I would have wanted it to be. But it wasn't anything I couldn't handle. This trip was about finding the things on the letters for these kids, ranging from as young as three to as old as fifteen, both boys and girls. It was going to be a challenge, some of them, but it was going to be worth it when they opened their gifts and saw the thing their letter had asked for.

Most of them anyway.

Our first stop was an obvious one. Myrna's World Of Play was one of the more unique places in the whole state. A huge store with two floors, Myrna's was absolutely chock-full of toys of every type. There were traditional toys like Barbies and action figures of the latest blockbuster movies alongside weird niche toys that you couldn't find anywhere else.

It was a delightful place to visit, even for adults, and the second we walked in I felt like a kid again. The store was rather packed with customers, the vast majority of them grown-ups. People came from several counties over to Myrna's, and framed articles along the wall near the entrance showed how famous the place had gotten across the state.

Thankfully we found a number of the toys we were looking for rather easily, and Lawson was predictably adorable in the store. He kept picking things up and playing with them, seeing how they worked and then that booming, gut laughter would fill the store. I looked forward to every time he laughed like that. It was so genuine, so real. So cheerful.

After purchasing what we found and bringing it all back to the car, we headed to the bakery across the street from Myrna's. Lawson guided me inside by the hand and I sighed when the smell of the fresh baked bread hit my nose. Suddenly I realized just how hungry I was, and remembered the dough in the refrigerator.

"You know, we should use that dough I have in the fridge to make something for the kids," I said.

"That would be awesome," Lawson said, getting in line. "But we don't have the time to go back and make something. I have an idea, though. What if we made an order here for delivery and we saved your dough for Christmas morning?"

"Would they take an order this close to the holiday?" I asked. "Everyone seems so busy."

"We can try. Maybe if we explain the situation to them," he said. "Hang on."

Lawson stepped out of line and I stayed in it, ordering both of us a sandwich and bringing it to the only empty table in the place. The bakery was unique in that it served all manner of food, including cakes and pies as well as deli sandwiches. There were two kitchens, a remnant of when it had been two restaurants side by side. One day, after years of being side by side, the children of the owners of both places ended up together and got married. They took over both places and combined them. It was a cute story, and I read the little biography on the back of the menus on the table while I waited for Lawson to return.

When he did, he was bringing an older gentleman with him, probably in his late fifties, wearing an apron covered in flour.

"Holly, meet Giuseppe Harris. Giuseppe, this is Holly."

"Nice to meet you," I said. "Is this your place?"

He nodded. "My wife's and mine," he said. "She runs the business. I just make bread and pie shells." He laughed, and the sound came out easy and musical. I got the impression by the laugh lines on his face and his kind eyes that he laughed a lot.

"Giuseppe offered to help us out tonight," Lawson said, beaming. "I told him what was going on and he said he can donate and help us out."

"What? That's amazing," I replied.

Giuseppe smiled warmly.

"I heard what Lawson said about the little children. I am closing the shop at five today, but I will stay and make some pastries and treats for the babies. Don't you worry."

We spent a few hours running around downtown, gathering other gifts and supplies. A trip into the candy shop ended up with a basket of goodies being donated by them, too. A few other businesses offered to pitch in, and even though it was extremely short notice it was like the town was coming together just for this.

I couldn't believe it. Everyone had been so generous, and had been so in the last second. Everyone wanted to spend time with their own families and provide for them over the holiday, yet we had several business owners offer their time in lieu of not having anything they could give us. The hospital was going to have an entire team showing up to help them finish decorating and run the event, as well as various places bringing things over.

We piled into the car, the backseat and trunk stuffed so much that Lawson couldn't see out the back window. We drove to the house and unloaded quickly, bringing everything into my room and spreading it out on the floor and the bed as we took inventory of what we had. The letters were on one side of the bed and I started placing each one in its own space in the room and gathering gifts that matched it on top of each one.

Lawson went downstairs and grabbed some coffee and cocoa and brought it up as we separated things out and then started building treat baskets, wrapping gifts, and bundling things together for each kid.

"Don't forget, we have to stop by four of the stores to pick stuff up before we head down there," Lawson said. "I think it might work out if we took both cars. Just so we have enough room for everything."

"Good idea," I said. "It will give me a few extra minutes to get ready before we head down."

"Perfect," he said. "Hey, this wrestling figure... was it Sam's or Ryder's?"

I looked at the figure and remembered the name of the wrestler being on Ryder's list. It was a rather eclectic list. While most kids seemed to have a theme for their gifts, Ryder was all over the place. Books, building toys, action figures, a basketball—his list included a whole host of items. We couldn't get them all, but we were able to find a bunch of them.

It was tricky because some of the kids didn't really give us a lot to go on. Their letters were basic and only had one or two items on it, while others had a list that unfurled like a CVS receipt. We had to make sure to disperse the gifts as evenly as we could, but it was going to be difficult since some of them asked for things that were easy to find and others asked for more difficult items.

The last stop had been to the comic book store, and I glanced over at the box of comics Lawson had grabbed. Quite a lot of them were the *Iron Man* comics he had gone in for, but the rest were just tossed in by the store owner when he heard what was happening. They ranged from newer issues of popular titles to some of the doubles of older issues he had in stock.

On a whim, I pulled them out and separated out all the ones Jerome would probably want and then dispersed the rest among all the other letters. Lawson watched me curiously, and when I put the last one down he cocked an eyebrow. I smiled.

"I thought that if we gave everybody a comic or two, they could get together and discuss them. It might help him make friends if everyone shares in his thing. Is that stupid?"

"Not at all," Lawson said. "That's really sweet, actually. And a great idea. I know when I was a kid, we often got together to brag about our hauls. If everyone got a comic book, it should help them all connect over it. Good call."

"Thank you," I said, smiling and looking around the room. "How much extra did we get?"

"We got a fair bit," he said. "I wanted to make sure we could put together some stuff for the parents and the siblings, too. I get the feeling that everyone could use a little Christmas cheer tonight. I also got a couple things for Rachael and the staff, too."

The children's hospital was one of the bigger buildings in the city in terms of square footage, but it was rivaled by the housing building next door. That unit had been a hotel once upon a time, but the city had claimed it when it went defunct years before. According to Rachael it was given to the Children's Hospital, and they spent a ton of time and money refurbishing it so they could allow the families to stay there while their children were getting treatment.

It was a nice place, but the biggest concern was always that the siblings of the kids who were there would get bored easily and feel left out. All the attention would be on their sick siblings, and they could feel invisible. There was always a concerted effort on the staff's part to make sure they were included in as many things as they could.

"Perfect," she said. "I was thinking we could put together a gift basket for them. Some fancy coffee or something?"

"Like the stuff you have downstairs that you refuse to touch, because it smells like donuts and you're afraid you'll subliminally want them and eat a dozen in a single sitting?" he teased.

"Yes," I said. "And now I regret telling you that."

"We can get some more at the coffee shop by Myrna's. I have to stop by there anyway."

"Good," I said. "I have one other idea."

"What's that?" he asked.

"My crocheting," I said. "I have stacks of hats and scarves that I have been making for a few months, with every intention on donating them at some point. But with everything that's happened with this place, I haven't gotten around to donating them anywhere. Do you think the families would enjoy them?"

"I absolutely think they would," he said, stepping close to me and wrapping me in a hug. "That would be wonderful. They would love that."

"I just thought it would be nice because I could donate them, and I would actually get the joy of seeing them get them directly. Usually when I donate things, it's anonymous. And it going to families and their children just makes it that much better. I always worry it will end up with some adult who thinks it's ugly and sticks it in a drawer somewhere where it will never get touched."

"They will love them," Lawson said. "Go get them and dole them out. We need to pack up and get ready if we're going to make it to the businesses that can't attend tonight and get what they're donating."

"Is Myrna coming?"

"She said she couldn't," Lawson smiled. "But I have my doubts."

"Me, too," I grinned.

Chapter Fifty-Nine

Lawson

Before we headed out, we went to our respective rooms to get ready. I had a plan that I was excited about and only needed something warm to wear in the meantime, but an ugly Christmas sweater I saw at one of our stops had called my name. Now it was on my body.

It looked terrible. Abjectly horrible. I loved it.

Garish and green with red stripes, and bells in various places, it was supposed to look like a Christmas tree. It looked as if a three-year-old had been given access to a seamstress and was allowed to put whatever they wanted on the sweater, no questions asked.

I stepped out of the room and went downstairs to wait for Holly, glad that I had already packed both cars with the presents. We still had a little bit of time, but it was quickly running out. There was still a stop or two to make on the way, and I was determined to get there early enough to see the kids when they were brought to the lobby.

The bag with my big plan was in my hand, and I twirled it a bit as I waited on Holly. It was going to be spectacular if I could pull it off. I had talked with Rachael about visits from Santa when we were there, and when I went into Myrna's I stumbled into the costume section and this one caught my eye.

It was a lifelong dream that I never knew I really had. Somewhere in the back of my mind, I guessed I always wanted to be Santa Claus. It was never a thing that I would have put together to really think about as a goal, but as soon as I saw the suit on the rack I knew it was my destiny. I had to be Santa.

My only worry was that I wouldn't have the body type the kids expected. That was why there was also a pillow in the bag with the costume. It might not work, but I wanted it just in case. Otherwise, the kids would have to get used to the idea of Santa with a six-pack.

Holly's door opened and I looked up the stairs at the sound of it. She stepped out and my jaw dropped. She looked incredible.

She was all dressed up for the party, in a red dress with white trim. Black buttons up the front made her look like the sexiest Mrs. Claus ever. She had a little white and red purse and red heels with white stockings. The hem of the dress stopped just above her knees, but the effect on me was intense anyway. Her hair cascaded down her shoulders and she had a jaunty little Santa hat on.

"Do I look all right?" she asked as she reached the bottom of the stairs. Her lipstick was shining in the light, and I was dying to ask for a taste.

"You look amazing," I said. "Seriously amazing."

"You have your bag ready?" she asked.

I held it up and waggled it a little.

"I won't look nearly as good in mine as you do in yours, but yes, I have it," I said.

"So," she said, "you're wearing the sweater."

"I am," I said. "For now."

"It's a choice."

"The right one." I beamed. She rolled her eyes, but her smile was still wide.

"Then let's get going. We have kids to make Christmas happen for."

I held out my arm and she hooked hers inside, and we began walking to the door.

Holly followed me as we drove to the two stops we needed to make and then to the hospital. We had done such a good job of getting things prepared and getting dressed quickly that she didn't need to meet me there. But we had so much stuff between the two cars there was no way we could fit it all in one.

As we pulled into the hospital parking lot, I saw Giuseppe's van out front. He must have already arrived and was still inside. I had a feeling he might stay for a little while, especially if he convinced his wife to come with.

I opened Holly's passenger door and helped her fill her arms with things to carry in and then went to mine to grab stuff from my car. When we got to the front door Rachael ran over to open it for us and let us inside, then grabbed her coat to come help us. It took several trips, but eventually we had everything in. Holly and Rachael were putting them in the office, where I could hide them until later. They decided to bring one gift out for each kid, putting it under the tree to start, and then I would come in later with everything else.

By the time they were done staging the area, the tree was ridiculously overflowing. Presents were stacked all around it, behind it, literally on it. It was impressive and heartwarming knowing that these kids were going to have a good time, and this was just the tip of the iceberg. The office was stuffed full of things, and I realized that some of the other business owners must have brought extras to add to the piles. Rachael said they had about ten minutes to get things ready before they went and fetched them, and several of the business owners who had come to help decorate used the time to change.

Giuseppe was in the kitchenette in the breakroom with his wife, making plates to hand out with cupcakes and pie slices. I ducked my head inside to say hello and he waved cheerfully at me. He was such a sweet man, and I was so happy I had run into him in the bakery.

Eventually, Rachael went to the hallway leading to the rooms and started bringing children in. As soon as they walked into the lobby, their jaws dropped and eyes lit up. The lobby looked fantastic now, such a dramatic change from where it had been that morning. Decorations were everywhere, garlands and lights and bows all over the place. Kids ran to the tree, which was decorated so perfectly it looked like it came right out of a magazine. They didn't reach for the presents but you could see them eyeing each one, looking for the nametags.

Before gifts got underway Rachael brought Giuseppe out and they handed out treats, and music began playing through the room. The atmosphere was festive and fun, and the parents who weren't out there to help decorate started filtering in as well, emotion washing over their faces. A few of them broke down, having to leave the room temporarily to gain a measure of control and then come back in, their eyes wet with tears and a smile on their face that I would have done anything to see.

It was more than just making these kids happy. Some of these kids would never see the inside of their homes again. Most of them would, but it would be a while, and even then it might be a tough life for them. For others this was a temporary stay; a disruption of their normal family routine, but not one that would last much longer. But for all of them, regardless of the diagnoses, it was hard to be here over the holidays.

There was fear, depression, and sadness that permeated being in this building even when hope was high. Even when the diagnosis was good and the time frame for recovery was low, somewhere in the building nearby, someone else was getting far worse news. It was impossible to ignore, and while the staff did the best they could it still seeped out.

But today, for one day, they could forget. They could let go of the sadness for one evening, let go of the worry and the pain. They could just enjoy a day of silly Christmas revelry. The children and, almost as importantly, the parents too.

Some of the kids were wheeled in, either in a chair or on their beds. I went to them first, knowing they couldn't just go join the others gathering around the tree. I wanted them to know all these strangers in the room were there for them. To give them a good holiday and wish them a happy new year. Some seemed to understand and spoke with me. Others only looked at me with eyes that were excited, but mouths that couldn't speak.

The treats were doled out, Giuseppe having thought ahead and called Rachael to see what alternatives he needed to make for special diets, leaving only a handful of the sugary cupcakes. When I was sure the children and parents and siblings had their fill, I walked them around to the other adults and passed them out. When I got back to Holly, who had been helping Rachael guide children to the crafts and art supplies laid out for them, I brought her the last cupcake.

She smiled when I presented it to her and she took it, unwrapping the paper and taking a small bite. Then she held it out to me and I took one of my own. A bit of icing got on my nose and she giggled. I stood up, wiping it off and laughing myself. A look from Rachael between us both told me she thought we were cute, and I didn't have any arguments. I was smitten with Holly.

Finally it was time for presents, and as the kids were handed the gifts for them under the tree, I used the distraction to sneak away. My idea was in motion.

I changed into my Santa suit, stuffing the pillow under my shirt, and snuck to the office to gather the gifts inside. Another parent met me in there and helped me load them all onto two gurneys push them to the edge of the lobby while all the children were facing the other way. Then he ran inside, tapped his daughter on the shoulder, and told her to turn around. She glanced back at me, peeking around the corner, and I winked.

"It's Santa!" she cried, and there was a confused sound of people looking around, many of the children toward the fireplace.

"Ho, ho, ho!" I shouted as I rounded the corner, pushing one gurney and pulling the other.

The room exploded in happy, excited sounds and I was suddenly surrounded by children, all cheering and being thrilled. I parked the gurney along one wall near the tree and gave hugs to any of the kids who wanted one. I spotted little Jerome and looked back at the presents wrapped on the beds. Finding the one I remembered wrapping myself, I grabbed it and handed it to him. He opened it and his face was alight as he saw the stack of *Iron Man* comics.

"How did you know?" he shouted.

"You wrote me a letter," I said. "And I never forget."

His jaw dropped to his chest as he looked back down to his comics, a look of pure joy on his face. It wasn't the only gift he got, but it was probably the first one he would remember each time he thought of that day. I loved knowing that I had a part in making that memory come alive in him for the rest of his life.

Holly came up beside me and started helping me hand out presents, the unmarked ones going to siblings or parents, depending on the paper they were wrapped in. I had a hard time keeping tears from welling up in my eyes as I watched the children have their wishes fulfilled as best we could.

It was the best moment I could remember having in a long, long time, and I was so happy to be sharing it with Holly.

Chapter Sixty

Holly

It was one of the best Christmas moments I have ever experienced. From the moment they brought the kids into the lobby, I felt overwhelmed with emotion. The joy on their faces as they ate treats that were made with all their various dietary needs in mind, took in the decorations that the employees and parents and business owners of the town had spent so much time putting together, was magic. Absolute magic.

Lawson looked happier than I have ever seen him when he came in dressed as Santa. There was a sparkle in his eyes, almost hidden between the white trim of his hat and the big, fluffy fake beard. The outfit looked a bit silly on him, considering he was so incredibly in shape, but that might have just been me because I knew what was under the suit. To everyone else, his towering presence and general bigness might have made up for the fact that you could tell pretty easily he had a pillow tied around his stomach.

The kids didn't seem to notice, and that was the only real worry. They were so enamored with him and how big and loud and in character he was that they didn't seem to be putting together the inconsistencies. For the rest of the adults, it was an incredible surprise. They were used to Santa making special appearances once a year or so, but usually at a distance or doing the lap-sitting deal. This was different. Lawson was personable and walking around, talking to them.

And he knew their names.

I was sure Rachael was helping him somehow, but it felt like magic. He would be able to pinpoint children and bring them their gifts personally, especially the ones who couldn't really move around much and were stuck in chairs or beds that had been wheeled in. Jerome, being first, was especially poignant since we had fretted over his letter and gifts so much. Seeing him completely believe was something I didn't think I would ever forget.

I tried to hang near Lawson the rest of the evening, helping him by carrying gifts for the kid he was going to see or talking with the parents while he spoke to the child. More than a few of them asked if I was Mrs. Claus, and after the second time of avoiding audibly confirming it I went with it and just told them I was. Lawson didn't seem to mind, and we kept moving through the kids one by one, talking about their letters and surprising them with as many of the gifts that were on them as we could.

As the revelry continued, Rachael pulled us both aside and asked us to make a video for the kids who weren't able to make it out of their rooms. I stayed quiet while he performed, showing off the gifts that he got for each person he filmed a video for and being shockingly good at the performance. If I didn't know any better, I would have said this wasn't the first time he had played Santa. But I watched him buy the suit and he talked briefly about how excited he was to do it, implying it was his first time.

He was a natural.

The treats were great, and Giuseppe outdid himself. The other food that had been brought in was nearly as good, and I spent the majority of the evening with a glass of sparkling grape juice in my hand. As the party started winding toward a close, Lawson pulled me aside and spoke quietly to me.

"We should make a big exit so the kids won't fight going back to their rooms. If I'm still here I'm afraid they will, fearing they'll be missing something," he said.

"Okay, how do you want to do it?"

Lawson grinned and looked toward the door, then took my hand.

"Come with me," he said.

"Okay."

We walked toward the front door and he pulled me to his side, still holding my hand, and faced us toward the crowd.

"Children! Sadly, it's time for Santa to go." A chorus of sad sounds came from the children and more than a few of the adults. "I know, I would like to stay here tonight with you as well. However, this time of year is rather busy for me, and I must be off to prepare. I hope everyone had a wonderful time and... what's this?"

He was looking above him and I turned to see what he was looking at. My heart jumped a little bit when I saw that directly above us hung mistletoe. I looked into his twinkling eyes, and for a moment the magic was real. He was Santa. I was Mrs. Claus. And there was an obligation to be met under the mistletoe.

"Why I think that's mistletoe, Santa," I said.

There was much mixed emotion and reactions from the children as Santa pulled me in tight and pressed his lips to mine. The fake beard tickled my upper lip a little, but I didn't care. The reaction of the kids, however, made the rest of us laugh and I broke down into giggles, breaking the kiss.

"With that," Lawson said, "we must be off! Merry Christmas to all, and to all a good night!"

Lawson tugged lightly on my hand and we swept our way out of the hospital, waving over our shoulders as the children waved back and shouted their own wishes for a Merry Christmas at us.

We ran around the side of the building and hopped into his car, letting mine stay at the hospital for the night. As we drove away, he pulled the beard off his face and set it down on the console between the seats. For the first time since he put it on, I could see his smile. It looked glued to his face.

"That was amazing," I said.

"Yes, it was," he said. "It really was. Seeing their little faces light up like that..."

He didn't have to finish the thought. I knew what he was saying. It was incredible, and gratifying to be able to bring joy to them, and any doubts I might have had about Christmas seemed like they slipped away during those hours. I turned into Mrs. Claus for the night. Literally.

We got back to the house a few minutes later, to find the main room was quiet. Most of the guests were either already off to bed or still out doing last-minute shopping or enjoying the lights in the park. Everything was dark and cozy, and all I wanted to do was get into pajamas and curl into him.

But not in the main room. I wanted him alone.

It was tricky, though, as was our whole situation. Asking him to come back to my room might mean that there was more expected of the situation, as would me going back to his. I didn't know how to express to him that I just wanted to be near him, to hold him through the night and listen to his heart beating in his chest as my head lay on it.

Our eyes met across the kitchen table as I made us a quick dinner of leftovers from the night before. There was a calmness in his eyes now. A satisfaction of a job well done, one he truly deserved.

"This chicken pot pie is delicious," he said. "You did really well with the pie dough."

"You can thank the bakery at the grocery store for that one," I said. When he cocked an eyebrow, I shrugged. "You weren't around to help me make one, and they had them on sale weeks ago. So I bought them and froze them."

"If you had frozen pie crusts, why did you keep trying to make your own from scratch?"

"I broke all but one of them before I started making them from scratch," I admitted. "I dropped them in the driveway and they shattered. One made it and I stuck it way back in the back of the freezer as a just-in-case."

He laughed and shook his head.

"Well, they did a fine job with the dough. You did great with the filling," I said.

"Thank you," I said, picking at my own plate. "I think I'm about done."

"Me too," he said. "I filled up on cupcakes and those little cinnamon bread things."

"Churros," I said. "They were churros."

"Right," he said. "I knew there was a name for them, I just forgot what it was. They were delicious."

"They were," I agreed. "I must have eaten three of them."

"Ahh, I got you beat," he laughed. "By a lot."

"How many?"

"A lot," he said, then we both laughed.

"All right Churro Claus, I think it's time to hit the sack," I said.

It was a tactical move, saying it that way. It implied that we would go to bed together without explicitly saying so. It still could mean we ended up in different rooms. However he took it, Lawson didn't give any indication of what that way was, and I frowned. Putting the dishes away, I started for the stairs and Lawson followed me.

As we got to the crest of the landing, Lawson pulled me in tight so our lips were barely touching.

"Earlier," he said. "Santa got a kiss from Mrs. Claus," he said.

"I remember."

"But I'm not Santa anymore," he said. "And there's no mistletoe. No obligation."

"I can see that," I said, my voice barely above a whisper as our lips inched closer and closer.

"So this is from me," he said.

Our lips met and I felt my body completely melt into him. He held me up, kissing me deeply, passionately, and then pulling away.

"Goodnight," he said, his lips brushing mine as he spoke.

"Wait," I said before he got more than two steps away.

"Yes?" he asked, turning back toward me.

"Stay with me tonight," I said.

He paused only for a moment, a small smile curling up one side of his face, then nodded.

"Let me go get my things."

I nodded and he went into his room. I went into mine, leaving the door cracked, and changed into pajamas. I didn't mean I wanted to have sex tonight, and I felt like he understood, maybe even agreed. Our emotions were running high after tonight, and crossing that line again might be something we would want to wait on until we were thinking a bit more clearly. And weren't as tired.

Lawson came into the room just as I opened the bathroom door. He settled his stuff on the counter and we brushed our teeth, side by side. When we were done with that, he went into the bedroom and I washed the makeup off my face, tying my hair behind me in a braid. When I got back into my room he was in the bed, only wearing a white t-shirt that I could see, the blankets over his stomach.

I smiled and crawled into the bed with him, grabbing the remote. I flipped on the television on the wall and navigated to the streaming channel with the baking show he loved so much. Putting on an episode, I put the remote down on the nightstand and settled into his arms. I didn't bother to watch the show at all, content to close my eyes and settle into sleep with him.

Soon, his breathing slowed and his heartbeat followed. I could hear the show just barely above it, but I focused on him. The smell of him. The feeling of his muscular chest under my head. The sound of the thumping in his ribcage.

And we drifted off together, slipping into a content and happy sleep. The last thing I remembered before dreams took over was him kissing me on the top of my head.

I dreamed of carriage rides and snowmen. I dreamed of Christmas.

THE END
of Part 10

Snowflake
HOLLOW
12 DAYS OF CHRISTMAS
ADVENT CALENDARS
3
12
7
5
10
9
2
4
6
1
8
11
NEW CHAPTER EVERY DAY

Find Lexy Timms:

LEXY TIMMS NEWSLETTER:
http://www.lexytimms/newsletter
Lexy Timms Facebook Page:
https://www.facebook.com/SavingForever
Lexy Timms Website:
http://www.lexytimms.com

Want

FREE READS?

Sign up for Lexy Timms' newsletter
And she'll send you updates on new releases,
ARC copies of books and a whole lotta fun!

Sign up for news and updates!
http://www.lexytimms/newsletter

Holiday Romance by Lexy Timms

LOVERS IN LONDON SERIES #6
Sparkling
CHRISTMAS
USA TODAY BESTSELLING AUTHOR
LEXY TIMMS

DRIVING HOME FOR
Christmas
USA TODAY BESTSELLING AUTHOR
LEXY TIMMS
LIMITED
TIME
Lexy
Timms
FREE
DOWNLOAD

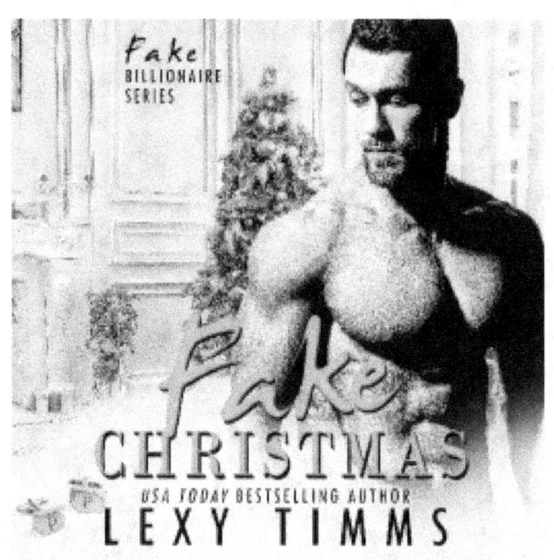

Don't miss out!

Visit the website below and you can sign up to receive emails whenever Lexy Timms publishes a new book. There's no charge and no obligation.

https://books2read.com/r/B-A-NNL-MAZTB

BOOKS 2 READ

Connecting independent readers to independent writers.

Did you love *Snowflake Hollow - Part 10*? Then you should read *Hades' Spawn MC Complete Series*[1] by Lexy Timms!

From Best Selling Author, Lexy Timms, comes a motorcycle club romance that'll make you want to buy a Harley and fall in love all over again.

<u>Book 1</u>

Emily Rose Dougherty is a good Catholic girl from mythical Walkerville, CT. She had somehow managed to get herself into a heap trouble with the law, all because an ex-boyfriend has decided to make things difficult.

Luke "Spade" Wade owns a Motorcycle repair shop and is the Road Caption for Hades' Spawn MC. He's shocked when he reads in the paper that his old high school flame has been arrested. She's always been the one he couldn't forget.

---

1. https://books2read.com/u/bMG7NA

2. https://books2read.com/u/bMG7NA

Will destiny let them find each other again? Or what happens in the past, best left for the history books?

<u>Book 2</u>

Emily Rose Dougherty had only fallen in love once, in high school with a boy her parents didn't approve of. Emily saw through the tough-guy façade, his leather jacket and motorcycle. She gave her heart to him. An accident on Luke's motorcycle brought things to a screeching halt when her parents forbade her to see him again. Neither forgot about the other. Fast forward ten years... Luke Wade built a good life as the owner of a motorcycle repair shop and the road captain of Hades' Spawn Motor Cycle Club. When he reconnects with his high school love, Emily, things seem to be falling into place. When dirty dealings within Hades' Spawn, problems created by Emily's ex-boyfriend and secrets from Luke's past threaten to blow Luke's life and his relationship with Emily apart, it suddenly feels like everything spiralling out of control. Can Luke and Emily find a way to conquer the obstacles to their love or will they be to each other, "the one that got away?"

<u>Book 3</u>

Emily Dougherty and Luke Wade were in love in high school, but circumstances conspired to keep them apart. Ten years later they meet again and find their connection is just as strong and more searingly hot than ever. Except Luke and his motorcycle club, Hades' Spawn, are hip deep in problems between the vicious Rojos one percenter motorcycle club and their associated street gang, the Hombres. When Luke's employee and best friend, Gibs, is slain in a brutal shootout, dark secrets from Luke's past claim him. He finds he has to make a deal with the devil just to keep Emily and his club safe. However, to keep Emily out of danger he must also to turn his back on her. Emily has lost her car, her job, and had to seek an order of protection against her ex, Evan Waters. In the face of her family's disapproval she's determined not to lose Luke too. But will Luke's heartless rejection drive her away? Or will she keep the faith and hope Luke finds his way back to her before her own secret causes her to do the unthinkable? Can Luke and Emily survive the hopeless tangle of club and gang politics, and the fierce reach of the law to find their way back to each other?

<u>Book 4</u>

Emily Dougherty and Luke Wade were in love in high school, but circumstances conspired to keep them apart. Ten years later they meet again and find their connection is just as strong and more searingly hot than ever. Events take a dangerous turn when Luke's uncle, Mexican drug lord Raymondo Icherra shows up and stirs up trouble. Emily's pregancy turns high risk with her fainting and having continuous high blood pressure. While Luke deals with a problem with his MC club Hades Spawn, Emily is kidnapped by persons unknown. As Luke searches frantically for Emily he learns the truth about his past and his parent's murder.

Read more at www.lexytimms.com.

Also by Lexy Timms

12 Days of Christmas
Snowflake Hollow - Part 1
Snowflake Hollow - Part 2
Snowflake Hollow - Part 3
Snowflake Hollow - Part 4
Snowflake Hollow - Part 5
Snowflake Hollow - Part 6
Snowflake Hollow - Part 7
Snowflake Hollow - Part 8
Snowflake Hollow - Part 9
Snowflake Hollow - Part 10

A Bad Boy Bullied Romance
I Hate You
I Hate You A Little Bit
I Hate You A Little Bit More

A Bump in the Road Series
Expecting Love
Selfless Act

Doctor's Orders

A Burning Love Series
Spark of Passion
Flame of Desire
Blaze of Ecstasy

A Chance at Forever Series
Forever Perfect
Forever Desired
Forever Together

A Dark Mafia Romance Series
Taken By The Mob Boss
Truce With The Mob Boss
Taking Over the Mob Boss
Trouble For The Mob Boss
Tailored By The Mob Boss
Tricking the Mob Boss

A Dating App Series
I've Been Matched
You've Been Matched
We've Been Matched

A "Kind of" Billionaire
Taking a Risk
Safety in Numbers
Pretend You're Mine

A Maybe Series
Maybe I Should
Maybe I Shouldn't
Maybe I Did

Assisting the Boss Series
Billion Reasons
Duke of Delegation
Late Night Meetings
Delegating Love
Suitors and Admirers

BBW Romance Series
Capturing Her Beauty
Pursuing Her Dreams
Tracing Her Curves

Beating the Biker Series
Making Her His

Making the Break
Making of Them

Betrayal at the Bay Series
Devil's Bay
Devil's Deceit
Devil's Duplicity

Billionaire Banker Series
Banking on Him
Price of Passion
Investing in Love
Knowing Your Worth
Treasured Forever
Banking on Christmas
Billionaire Banker Box Set Books #1-3

Billionaire CEO Brothers
Tempting the Player
Late Night Boardroom
Reviewing the Perfomance
Result of Passion
Directing the Next Move
Touching the Assets

Billionaire Hitman Series

The Hit
The Job
The Run

Billionaire Holiday Romance Series
Driving Home for Christmas
The Valentine Getaway
Cruising Love
Billionaire Holiday Romance Box Set

Billionaire in Disguise Series
Facade
Illusion
Charade

Billionaire Secrets Series
The Secret
Freedom
Courage
Trust
Impulse
Billionaire Secrets Box Set Books #1-3

Blind Sight Series
See Me
Fix Me

Eyes On Me

Branded Series
Money or Nothing
What People Say
Give and Take

Building Billions
Building Billions - Part 1
Building Billions - Part 2
Building Billions - Part 3

Butler & Heiress Series
To Serve
For Duty
No Chore
All Wrapped Up

Change of Heart Series
The Heart Needs
The Heart Wants
The Heart Knows

Counting the Billions
Counting the Days

Counting On You
Counting the Kisses

Cry Wolf Reverse Harem Series
Beautiful & Wild
Misunderstood
Never Tamed

Darkest Night Series
Savage
Vicious
Brutal
Sinful
Fierce

Diamond in the Rough Anthology
Billionaire Rock
Billionaire Rock - part 2

Dirty Little Taboo Series
Flirting Touch
Denying Pleasure
Forbidding Desire
Craving Passion

Dominating PA Series
Her Personal Assistant - Part 1
Her Personal Assistant - Part 2
Her Personal Assistant Box Set

Fake Billionaire Series
Faking It
Temporary CEO
Caught in the Act
Never Tell A Lie
Fake Christmas
Fake Billionaire Box Set #1-3

Firehouse Romance Series
Caught in Flames
Burning With Desire
Craving the Heat
Firehouse Romance Complete Collection

Forging Billions Series
Dirty Money
Petty Cash
Payment Required

For His Pleasure
Elizabeth
Georgia
Madison

Fortune Riders MC Series
Billionaire Biker
Billionaire Ransom
Billionaire Misery
Fortune Riders Box Set - Books #1-3

Fragile Series
Fragile Touch
Fragile Kiss
Fragile Love

Great Temptation Series
The Devil's Footsteps
Heaven's Command
Mortals Surrender

Hades' Spawn Motorcycle Club
One You Can't Forget
One That Got Away

One That Came Back
One You Never Leave
One Christmas Night
Hades' Spawn MC Complete Series

Hard Rocked Series
Rhyme
Harmony
Lyrics

Heart of Stone Series
The Protector
The Guardian
The Warrior

Heart of the Battle Series
Celtic Viking
Celtic Rune
Celtic Mann
Heart of the Battle Series Box Set

Heistdom Series
Master Thief
Goldmine
Diamond Heist
Smile For Me

Your Move
Green With Envy
Saving Money

Highlander Wolf Series
Pack Run
Pack Land
Pack Rules

Hollyweird Fae Series
Inception of Gold
Disruption of Magic
Guardians of Twilight

How To Love A Spy
The Secret
The Secret Life
The Secret Wife

Just About Series
About Love
About Truth
About Forever
Just About Box Set Books #1-3

Rough Sea
High Tide

Lovers in London Series
Risking Millions
Venture Capital
Worth the Expense
The Price of Luxury
Exclusive Passion
Lovers in London - 3 Book Box Set

Love You Series
Love Life
Need Love
My Love

Managing the Billionaire
Never Enough
Worth the Cost
Secret Admirers
Chasing Affection
Pressing Romance
Timeless Memories
Managing the Billionaire Box Set Books #1-3

Managing the Bosses Series

The Boss
The Boss Too
Who's the Boss Now
Love the Boss
I Do the Boss
Wife to the Boss
Employed by the Boss
Brother to the Boss
Senior Advisor to the Boss
Forever the Boss
Christmas With the Boss
Billionaire in Control
Billionaire Makes Millions
Billionaire at Work
Precious Little Thing
Priceless Love
Valentine Love
The Cost of Freedom
Trick or Treat
The Night Before Christmas
Gift for the Boss - Novella 3.5
Managing the Bosses Box Set #1-3
Managing the Bosses Novellas

Mislead by the Bad Boy Series
Deceived
Provoked
Betrayed

Model Mayhem Series

Shameless
Modesty
Imperfection

Moment in Time
Highlander's Bride
Victorian Bride
Modern Day Bride
A Royal Bride
Forever the Bride

Mountain Millionaire Series
Close to the Ridge
Crossing the Bluff
Climbing the Mount

My Best Friend's Sister
Hometown Calling
A Perfect Moment
Thrown in Together

My Darker Side Series
Darkest Hour
Time to Stop
Against the Light

Neverending Dream Series
Neverending Dream - Part 1
Neverending Dream - Part 2
Neverending Dream - Part 3
Neverending Dream - Part 4
Neverending Dream - Part 5
Neverending Dream Box Set Books #1-3

Outside the Octagon
Submit
Fight
Knockout

Protecting Diana Series
Her Bodyguard
Her Defender
Her Champion
Her Protector
Her Forever
Protecting Diana Box Set Books #1-3

Protecting Layla Series
His Mission
His Objective
His Devotion

Racing Hearts Series
Rush
Pace
Fast

Regency Romance Series
The Duchess Scandal - Part 1
The Duchess Scandal - Part 2

Reverse Harem Series
Primals
Archaic
Unitary

Roommate Wanted Series
The Roommate

R&S Rich and Single Series
Alex Reid
Parker
Sebastian

Saving Forever

Saving Forever - Part 1
Saving Forever - Part 2
Saving Forever - Part 3
Saving Forever - Part 4
Saving Forever - Part 5
Saving Forever - Part 6
Saving Forever Part 7
Saving Forever - Part 8
Saving Forever Boxset Books #1-3

Secrets & Lies Series
Strange Secrets
Evading Secrets
Inspiring Secrets
Lies and Secrets
Mastering Secrets
Alluring Secrets
Secrets & Lies Box Set Books #1-3

Shifting Desires Series
Jungle Heat
Jungle Fever
Jungle Blaze

Sin Series
Payment for Sin
Atonement Within
Declaration of Love

Happily Ever After

Tattooist Series
Confession of a Tattooist
Surrender of a Tattooist
Heart of a Tattooist
Hopes & Dreams of a Tattooist

Tennessee Romance
Whisky Lullaby
Whisky Melody
Whisky Harmony

The Bad Boy Alpha Club
Battle Lines - Part 1
Battle Lines

The Brush Of Love Series
Every Night
Every Day
Every Time
Every Way
Every Touch
The Brush of Love Series Box Set Books #1-3

The City of Mayhem Series
True Mayhem
Relentless Chaos
Broken Disorder

The Debt
The Debt: Part 1 - Damn Horse
The Debt: Complete Collection

The Fire Inside Series
Dare Me
Defy Me
Burn Me

The Gentleman's Club Series
Gambler
Player
Wager

The Golden Game
On The Pitch
Respect the Game
All Game
Sweat and Tears

The Final Score

The Golden Mail
Hot Off the Press
Extra! Extra!
Read All About It
Stop the Press
Breaking News
This Just In
The Golden Mail Box Set Books #1-3

The Lucky Billionaire Series
Lucky Break
Streak of Luck
Lucky in Love

The Millionaire's Pretty Woman Series
Perfect Stranger
Captive Devotion
Sweet Temptations

The Sound of Breaking Hearts Series
Disruption
Destroy
Devoted

Stormy Love
Savage Love
Secure Love

Worth It Series
Worth Billions
Worth Every Cent
Worth More Than Money

You & Me - A Bad Boy Romance
Just Me
Touch Me
Kiss Me

Standalone
Wash
Loving Charity
Summer Lovin'
Love & College
Billionaire Heart
First Love
Frisky and Fun Romance Box Collection
Beating Hades' Bikers
Everyone Loves a Bad Boy
Dead of Night

Watch for more at www.lexytimms.com.

About the Author

"Love should be something that lasts forever, not is lost forever." Visit USA TODAY BESTSELLING AUTHOR, LEXY TIMMS https://www.facebook.com/SavingForever *Please feel free to connect with me and share your comments. I love connecting with my readers.* Sign up for news and updates and freebies - I like spoiling my readers! http://eepurl.com/9i0vD website: www.lexytimms.com Dealing in Antique Jewelry and hanging out with her awesome hubby and three kids, Lexy Timms loves writing in her free time. MANAGING THE BOSS-ES is a bestselling 10-part series dipping into the lives of Alex Reid and Jamie Connors. Can a secretary really fall for her billionaire boss?

Read more at www.lexytimms.com.